Being Healthy

Book*Squirrel* Publication

Book*Squirrel* Publication

Regd. Under MSME Act.

"Being Healthy"

By: Kiran Suman

ISBN: 978-93-89557-87-9

Language

1st Edition

Formatting: Mr_Ash

Cover: Mr_Ash

<u>ACKNOWLEDGEMENT-</u>

Having an idea and turning it into a book is as hard as it sounds. The experience is both internally challenging and rewarding. I especially want to thank the individuals that helped make this happen.

Complete thanks to—

My papa

My maa

My younger brother Shubham

My partner Mukesh ji

My whole publishing team

A special thanks to my readers

I want to thank EVERYONE who ever said anything positive to me or taught me something. I heard it all, and it meant something.

<u>Ayurveda says-</u>

Sama dosha sama agnischa sama dhatu mala kriyaaha//
Prasanna atma indriya manaha swastha iti abhidheeyate//

--- Sushruta Samhita

- <u>The above mentioned phrase means-</u>

Just get up in the morning, you eat well, you shit well, you sleep well, you love well and you hate no one then you cannot have any disease.

One is perfectly healthy when three doshas (Vata, pitta, Kapha) digestive system (digestion, assimilation and metabolism) all the body components (dhatus like blood, plasma etc.) all the excretory functions are in order with contended mind, senses and spirit.

- <u>Then the question arises, how do you get the disease?</u>

Just because of Krodha (anger), Vaya (fear), Virudhana Bhojanam (wrong type of food at the wrong time), and Soka (sorrow), Alasya (laziness or sedentary lifestyle).

It is a simple idea that optimizing nutrition i.e. safe and a viable way to avoid, treat or lessen mental illness. After all nutrition matters. If we take any class of medications like antipsychotics, antidepressants, anti-anxiety drugs in the short term these medications are very effective but in a long term they are not and in some cases they are life-threatening also.

Everyone is contrasting. Everyone is distinct. All medical sciences work on averages. We have to understand the restriction of averages. In fact, modern treatments are very useful for emergency purpose, but not for everyday life on a long-term basis.

CONTENTS-

4. MEDICINES ARE HEALTHY?

5. TAKE FOOD AS MEDICINE
HUNGER
CHEWING
TASTE VS NUTRITION
QUANTITY OF FOOD VS ENERGY
CHILLED FOODS
ORGANIC FOODS
CONSEQUENCES OF HEATING
PLASTIC FOOD
MICRONUTRIENTS
MILK
SPROUTS
ACIDIC VS ALKALINE FOODS
SUGAR, SALT AND FAT
CURD IN WINTER??

6. FOOD THERAPY
CHOOSE RIGHT TEA
LISTEN TO YOUR BODY
DIET TIPS
NUTRACEUTICALS
GO WITH YOUR GUT FEELING
PROBIOTICS

7. IMPACT OF CHANGE

8. RIGOROUSLY CHANGE IN LIFESTYLE
PAY ATTENTION TO YOUR BODY
PAY ATTENTION TO FOOD LABELS
LAUGHTER IS THE BEST MEDICINE
A RIGHT STEP
SUNNYSIDE UP

9. EFFECTIVE DIET PLAN

10. HEALTH IS WEALTH

"Being healthy and fit is not a trend. Instead, it is a lifestyle."

Your future depends on not just your body but also on your mind. It's not what you eat that kills you; it is what eats you that kill you i.e. your negative thoughts, your negative attitude, your negative environment. All diseases that come because of the mind. Diseases originate in the mind, develop in the mind, spread in the mind and kill you in the mind.

If mothers want their child to have a healthy life they should implant good habits since childhood. If you sit, you shorten your lifespan; if you exercise you lengthen your lifespan. You decide how you want to live your precious life.

When people talk about health, they usually refer to the condition of the body. However, health doesn't merely mean being free from physical pain or the symptoms of the disease. The mind is of pivotal consideration in the overall appraisal of wellbeing.

A human being is a composite unit of five sheaths. The ancient Ayurveda health system propounded this truth more than five thousand years ago when it emphasized the importance of a balanced life, taking into consideration not only the body but also the mind and the soul. Indeed, the wisdom of Ayurveda is profound and enduring, as it heals the body, mind and soul. It gives knowledge of hygiene attributes and lifestyle that induce total health system.

ELIMINATION OF TOXINS

1. <u>ELIMINATION OF TOXINS-</u>

A healthy body is capable of eliminating the toxic substances generated by its normal functioning process. The liver plays a great role in the conversion and detoxification of toxins and is a vital organ in the eliminatory process. If the production of toxic metabolites overwhelms the limit it starts accumulating in the body, where the realization comes too late.

If we put a frog in a bucket of hot water, the frog will try to jump out. If the frog is put in a bucket of hot water at room temperature, and heat is applied gradually to it, it stays there till it is too late. In our case, we seem to have got habituated to live with all the unnatural lifestyles. Even then we suppress the signs and symptoms. Even sometimes we know the reason behind the cause then also we are continuing to do the same. Somehow we got habituated to live with all the abnormalities.

(a)<u>LIQUID TOXINS-</u>

Liquid toxins can be removed through urination and sweat. Air-conditioning prevents toxin elimination from the body by sweat. We must drink 2 to 3 litres of water daily. Quantity water is a necessary component of every bodily function. Adequate water intake allows toxin to be taken away from the cells and transported to the kidney to be excreted. Quality of water is also important for proper elimination. Properly filtered or spring water is important to decrease toxic effect. Any liquid intake is not same as water intake.

The right time to drink water is after waking up from the bed, it cleanses all your body parts, rehydrates your brain and helps in activating organs. Drinking water before a shower will help to lower the blood pressure. Drinking water after breakfast helps in neutralizing pH and acts as an immunity booster. Drinking water before our mid-day meal will help to dilute all our digestive juices tends to proper digestion and burns extra fat. Drinking water after lunch helps in preventing premature ageing. Drinking water before dinner helps in preventing overeating. Drinking water before going to bed will keep our body hydrated all night and will avoid heart problems.

Drinking lemon water on an empty stomach improves skin health, prevents colds and flu, promotes weight loss, relieves constipation and boosts metabolism.

Drinking water from a Copper cup lowers the risk of cancer, kill bacteria and regulate the functioning of the thyroid gland.

Nowadays it is common that green tea is very good for health. But it is also a fact that when you buy something from the market in a package, it contains some sort of preservatives to increase its shelf life. And silicon packing is very harmful to your body. So instead of buying the preservatives, you can also make some tea at home.

Preparation-

For this, you need some natural ingredients that are easily available in our kitchen.
Those are –

Half cup of Basil leaves
Few Pudina leaves
A small piece of ginger
A small piece of cinnamon
2 to 3 cloves
A small piece of fresh turmeric root
1 tsp honey
Lemon juice

Crush all the ingredients. Boil one and a half cup of water and add these crushed herbs to the water. Let the water simmer for a few minutes. Turn off the flame. Cover it for few minutes so that all the flavours merge with the water thoroughly.

Now strain the tea and add honey and lemon juice as per your taste. Drink it warm. This not only tastes great but also very much healthier for our body.

The combination of tulsi, ginger, ghee, honey and turmeric has been known to help cold. Tulsi is known to resolve cough. Cinnamon and lemon adds taste and also removes extra fat from our body. Turmeric and honey have antiseptic qualities. So these are much healthier that we can find in everyone's kitchen. Indian homes always have been a treasure of ancient wisdom. The instances may be many, but the fact is that people heal when they listen to their own body, what message it is radiating.

(b) <u>SOLID TOXINS-</u>

Solid toxins removed through stool. Whole foods like fruits, vegetables, dietary fibre have a low toxin concentration and are better for the body. While processed, packaged foods are difficult for the body to eliminate. Organic food decreases your exposure to toxins and puts less stress on body. Avoid canned foods. One motion for one meal is ideal. Quick, smooth and effortless elimination are good signs of clean colon. Look at your tongue, if colon is clean, no deposits on tongue i.e. not necessary to clean it. By **"HYDROTHERAPY"** also one can wash colon.

Hydrotherapy also called water therapy is done by applying three forms of water i.e. liquid, steam and ice. The prime goal of Hydrotherapy is to improve circulation and quality of blood. By improving the quality of blood, toxins can be eliminated more efficiently and more nutrients and minerals get reached to the target.

(C)GASEOUS TOXINS-

Pranayama is control of breath. Let's have a quick look at the word itself. 'Prana' stands for life force, while 'Yama' means control. According to classical yogic texts, prana is the energy of the universe. Through breathing we can control its intake. Breathing is regenerative and restorative. It can cleanse us of toxins that have built up in the body and mind. Gaseous toxins removed through breathing. Breathing high in the chest does not allow for optimal oxygenation of lungs, which can cause lack of oxygenation to the tissues. Learning to breadth deeply into the lower lungs through diaphragmatic breathing is an essential part of proper oxygenation of tissues and toxin elimination.

• ART OF BREATHING-

Full and free breathing is one of the most powerful keys to enhancing physical, emotional and spiritual wellbeing. We know breathing is important for our mind and body. This mind is just like a computer when there is lots of data in it, it becomes very slow. So we need to clear these files to run better. Our mind is also like a computer where there are lots of thoughts on it, it becomes very slow. And this breathing technique will help you to clean your thoughts to lead your life in a better way.

- ## **PROCESS-**

If you are sitting on a chair then spread your legs, your spine upright and concentrating on the outgoing breath by closing your eyes. Start deep breathing then breathe lightly and then relax. Do it up to five minutes will give you a great start in the morning.

Lung volume for an average person is five litres, but most people inhale one litre. As a result quality of air in lungs is dirty. Pranayam emphasis on cleaning toxins.

The correct way to breath is to inhale like a newborn baby.

(d)**YOGIC KRIYAS-**

Rishis did Maha Shankh Prakshalan before tapas, with a totally clean system, no food, few inhales, metabolism came to standstill. Ageing process stopped.

PROCESS-

Drink warm salt water of about one to two glasses and perform some asanas or exercises. Repeat this technique up to three times. It will gently wash the colon and clear water comes at the end. Shat Kriyas or Yogic cleansing processes are an integral part of yoga as they eliminate toxins from body. Body functions like a machine and it has to be cleaned rhythmically.

Six cleansing processes are—

1- <u>NETI</u>-

For upper nasal tract (from throat to nostrils)
Neti cleans and clears the nasal passage. This is of two types- Jalaneti and Sutraneti.

2- <u>KAPALBHATI</u>-

For lower respiratory tract (nostrils to lungs)
Jalaneti should be followed by proper drying of nose and exhaling forcefully, as any water residue can cause cold.

3- <u>DHAUTI</u>-

(For digestive tract up to stomach)-
Dhauti is a very important technique of auto cleansing.

4- <u>NAULI</u>-

(For abdominal muscles and internal organs)-
This yogic technique massages the entire abdomen by contracting and isolating the belly (abdomen) muscles.

5- <u>BASTI</u>-

(For lower digestive tract rectum)-
This is of two types – Jal Basti and Sthal Basti

6- <u>SHANKH PRAKSHALANA-</u>
(For entire GIT)
It washes the entire alimentary tract with water.

Mainly Jalaneti, Laghu Shankh Prakshalan, Sutra, Vastra dhouti are preferable.

(e) <u>FASTING-</u>

Fasting serves as a healthy way of detoxing. Fasting for health is not like modern days fasting for religious rituals. For detoxification, one has to live for a few days on the water or on liquid food. Naturally solid food has to be light food. Like first day only liquid, second day fast, third-day liquid and fourth-day solids (four days cycle). Herbal teas are also preferable.

LIFESTYLE

2. <u>LIFESTYLE-</u>

"The trick to making your lifestyle healthier is to make small healthy changes every day, such as taking the stairs instead of lifts, drinking one extra glass of water, increasing your fruit by one."

(a)<u>EATING OUT-</u>

Eating out is so common these days as it is always prone to poor nourishment and bad hygiene. The entire establishment for eating out gets business based on taste and not on nutrition. One is not even sure of their cooking medium and how long it has been used before changing.

(b)   <u>COLOUR ME-</u>

To make sure you are getting a variety of nutrients, vitamins and minerals into your body every day. Be the artist of your meals and paint a colour picture with a variety of yellow, red and green fruits and vegetable throughout the day.

(c) <u>STAY HEALTHY WITHOUT EXERCISE-</u>

If we walk instead of using a car, go up the stairs instead of using lifts, add protein in your diet, chew your food as many time as you can, drink plenty of water, avoid sitting of more than 30 minutes at a time, wipe floors etc. we do not need to exercise specifically.

Increase the essence of a standard of life than standard of living.

(d)   <u>HIGH HEELS-</u>

Though high heels are stylish, that can cause major problems for both your feet and your budget. Do not use high heels; it can cause natural posture deformation, pressure on bones, restricted movement, and sprain in ankles, lower back pain etc.

(e) <u>PORTION DISTORTION-</u>

Eat your main meals off a smaller plate- visually the plate looks full so you will be satisfied, but technically you will be eating less. Eat small regular meals (at least every four hours), so that you are never starving.

(f) <u>SWEET ENOUGH-</u>

From sugary drinks to breakfast cereals, it's hard to get away from sugary foods. The easiest way to limit your sugar intake with one small change is to cut out sugary fizzy drinks. This one will help you to lose weight, reduce heart disease risk, obesity and diabetes.

(g)<u>SITTING POSTURE VS BLOOD FLOW-</u>

In the older days, we used to work by sitting in a cross-legged position. Nowadays everyone since childhood sits on a chair. All our active organs are above the abdomen. While sitting on a chair, lot of blood flows to feet unnecessarily. So that all the needed organs including brain get less blood supply. It is good to sit in Vajrasana after meal to allow more blood supply to organs.

(h)   <u>TAKE A STAND FOR HEALTH-</u>

We spend our lives sitting at our chairs, in front of the TV, in a meeting or on the phone. So break your sitting time by standing for five minutes, and reap the health benefits. Every little bit counts and it all adds up to burning more calories.

(i) <u>EXERCISE-</u>

Exercise is therapy. "Those who cannot find time for exercise will have to find time for illness." Actually it can be supplemented as – "those who cannot find time for detoxifying will have to find time for illness".Remember that any exercise is better than no exercise.

- **<u>Benefits of walking thirty minutes a day-</u>**

Prevents obesity
Reduces stress level
Increases your energy level
Improves the quality of life
Improves coordination and balance
Helps to maintain weight
Reduces the risk of heart disease
Helps to boost mood
Helps to boost the immune system
Increases functioning of lungs

Walking adds creativity
Strengthens bones and muscles
Increases body's access to vitamin-D
Improves blood pumping
Reduces the risk of cancer
Maintains blood pressure
Improve the quality of sleep
Reduces anxiety

(j) <u>CANCER CAN BE CURED?</u>

Cells have a nucleus, that has DNA (blueprint) any damage to the blueprint can cause cancer and the damage can be caused by radiation, chemo toxin and by replication error by itself. But there are three safeguards to replace the damage.

1- DNA repair mode by itself.
2- If it is too much – apoptosis is followed (cell commit suicide)
3- If both of the above are not working – they go to senescence i.e. they do not divide any more.

And if all three fails and the cells with damaged DNA start living and growing can cause cancer.

No disease including cancer can exist in an alkaline environment. Tumour cells obtain the energy required for their existence in two ways-

1. By respiration (needs oxygen)
2. By fermentation (anaerobic process)

IN RESPIRATION- they burn organic materials to CO_2 and H_2O and IN FERMENTATION- they split glucose to lactic acid. Both CO_2 and lactic acids are acidic, means cancer cells essentially thrive in an acidic medium.

Every cancer can be cured up to 16 weeks, but the body has to be alkaline and oxygen-rich. You get the body to a healing pH level that is 7.6 pH is ideal.

In market chemically created vitamin-E also available but that is not that much durable as nature does.

"If nature creates the problem, nature creates the solution".

Eating more alkaline foods, like fresh fruits, vegetables and whole grains, vegan diet, a raw diet can improve overall health and well being. Staying hydrated, well-rested and breathing deeply can also improve the condition. Two most powerful tools for alkalizing body include lemon juice and baking soda. Lemon juice can actually be used to make water more alkaline.

• <u>CANCER-FIGHTING DRINK-</u>

Two spoons of freshly squeezed lemon juice or organic apple cider vinegar
½ tablespoon baking soda

Combine the baking soda into a tall glass containing lemon juice until it stops fizzing. Pour water into the glass. Then drink this in the morning on an empty stomach.

A DISEASE FREE HEALTH

3. <u>A DISEASE FREE HEALTH-</u>

A disease-free healthy body is not muscular body of gym, inner immunity gives it. Take care of your body. It's the only place you have to live.

(a)<u>CAUSES OF DISEASE-</u>

INHERITANCE
OWN LIFESTYLE

Inheritance is also due to inherited lifestyle. It's widely recognised that there is a direct correlation between poor levels of physical fitness and increased risk of chronic diseases.

The disease mainly caused by accumulation of toxins, and by taking medicines we try to suppress it rather than eradicate it. There is no pill for every ill but there is an ill following every ill. Immunity is affected by lifestyle. Western children have much lower level of immunity than Indian children, who live in more unhygienic conditions. Too clean homes are not good for children.

When we are young our body systems, processes, mechanisms are very much strong, as one tends to cope with wrong habits all systems get imbalanced and cannot cope with at a later age. Stop bad practices before they tend to become part of your lifestyle.Lifestyle diseases affect all age groups. Physical activity is the core behind this. Risk can be reduced by minor change in daily habits. Eating right is needed to keep disease at a bay.

(b) <u>**EXTERNAL VS INTERNAL HYGIENE-**</u>

Some emphasis on the cleaning of their visual parts, while some aware of the internal cleaning of their body. Actually we need to learn how to improve internal hygiene. Mothers need to inculcate internal cleanliness habits from childhood.

In today's world, people are so stressed out, if you are not able to sit 10 minutes a day without any disturbance to eat your food, then you are doing a stupid profession. All the great people in the world are very disciplined on two things i.e. personality and food; the way they ate it, how they ate it and when they ate it.

When you chew your food, the brain takes signal from your saliva(wherein mouth carbohydrates got digested) by saying that this man is eating certain thing so it will secrete proper acids according to the food is being eaten. So proper digestion will be done. But we actually gulf our food without giving enough information to the brain. Then the food doesn't get digested in time, it becomes toxic. The stomach is just like our second brain, it can understand how to take care of the body. When the food is gulf down, small intestine is unable to digest it completely, so it pushes all the undigested food to the large intestine. Then we get a little belly and it becomes hard and swollen up. Here the flow of blood and nutrition is very minimum and your body is unhealthy now.

PRECAUTIONS ARE-

You finished eating your food at least three hours before you go to sleep. Blood is in the digestive system all the time when you lie down in sleeping position, the blood is kept there and is meant to digest the food quickly and rush to brain. The moment you eat the food just before you go to sleep, the brain says forgot me and all the blood let it be in the gut and just digest the food and if it not got digested it becomes toxic in four hours. So the needed amount of blood will not go to the brain. So the entire rejuvenating system of brain will fail.

So, you should 32 times chew your food and don't eat food after 7 to 8 PM.

MEDICINES ARE HEALTHY?

4. <u>MEDICINES ARE HEALTHY?</u>

There is no pill for every ill but there is an ill following every pill. If we take one medicine today, we will need more tomorrow. You may continue to take pills for lifelong, a pill will check that you do not become obese. If you stop, you will gain back the lost weight. The common perspective is that you take medicines as food in a regular manner; we are there to look after. No one is concerned for a disease-free body i.e. takes food as medicine.

TAKE FOOD AS MEDICINE

5. <u>TAKE FOOD AS MEDICINE-</u>

"Eat the way nature wants you to eat".

There are many reasons why we should pay attention to what we eat. The processed, low variety foods many of us consume regularly may be convenient and tasty, but they compromise our health. Overall, seeing your food as medicine helps you make better decisions about what and how to eat in order to make the best decisions for your own well being.

(a)<u>HUNGER-</u>

Hunger is when your mouth starts watering at the most tasteless foods. Do we eat when well hungry or by the watch? We eat even when we are not hungry. Please train yourself whether you eat when you are hungry or by watching.

(b)   <u>CHEWING-</u>

Chewing is very important for the proper absorption of food. We should chew our food at least 32 times, but it depends on food, ex- boiled food cannot be chewed up to 32 times while fibrous/ whole foods can be chewed more than 32 times. When food stays in the mouth for longer period, taste gets dissolved, to get the new bite for better taste. Our saliva is almost neutral. Saliva may help disinfect the food. Mother's concept is that the more and fast the child eats the better for him. At that time she unable to taught to chew. As a result child learns to gulp faster.

Your brain needs time to process that you have had enough to eat. Chewing your food thoroughly makes you eat very slowly which tends to increased fullness, decreased portion size, decreased food intake. Eating your food slowly can help you to feel full with little calorie.

How quickly you finish your meals may affect your weight. A recent survey reported that faster eaters are more likely to gain weight than slower eaters. Fast eaters are also more likely to be obese.

To get into the habit of eating more slowly, may help to count how many times you chew your bite.

(c) <u>TASTE VS NUTRITION-</u>

Now, this is a continuum of choice from taste vs. nutrition. It is not strictly either/or. Choosing foods based on nutritional value can help you avoid low-quality foods that harm and replace them with nutrient-dense foods that support healthy bodies. We are so used to pleasing the taste buds that we barely consider nutrients when we choose what to eat. Never in history have we seen such high levels of obesity, nutrient deficiency, chronic illness and diseases. Nutritious food may not always be tasty ex- karela, neem. When one tries pizza, cold drinks, chips, he/she doesn't find it tasty. This applies more to alcohol and smoking. But people adapt to taste of these things, we should adapt to the taste of healthy foods mostly.

(d) QUANTITY OF FOOD VS ENERGY-

Quantity of food is definitely a factor for obtaining energy. When the child is sick mothers want to feed the child whatever quantity is possible, so the child gets at least some food. 'Food during illness feeds the disease, not the patient'.

(e) CHILLED FOODS-

Digestion is a metabolically chemical process. All the chemical reactions slow down at minimum temperature. So by eating chilled food, it slows down the digestion process. Chilled water solidifies fat after each meal and making them more difficult to digest for the body. It can also restrict normal digestion, leads to constipation.
Ex- ice-cream, chilled water, cold drinks.

(f) <u>ORGANIC FOOD</u>-

'To eat is a necessity, but to eat intelligently is an art'.

Organic foods often have more beneficial nutrients, such as antioxidants, than their conventionally grown foods. Organic food is safer, more nutritious and often having better tasting than non-organic food. Organic production is better for the environment and kinder to animals. The researchers found that organic food had a 30% lower risk of pesticide residues but the residue levels on the conventional foods as well as within safety limits.

KNOW THE CLEAN 15-

The environmental working group have released a list called the "Clean 15"naming the least pesticide-ridden vegetables. If you can't afford to buy all organic then these you can buy - avocado, sweet corn, pineapple, cabbage, frozen peas, onion, asparagus, mango, papaya, kiwi, eggplant, grapefruit, cantaloupe, cauliflower and sweet potato.

(g) <u>CONSEQUENCES OF HEATING-</u>

- How long can you keep cooked food?
  For a few hours.
- How long will raw fruits and vegetables last?
  For a few days.
- What happens to sprouts every day after germination?
  They are growing daily.

A boiled seed doesn't germinate. There is no change in the chemistry of food by boiling.

We all consider CHEENA to be healthy milk product. It is considered light but MAWA is considered to be a heavy milk product and is difficult to digest also. For making CHEENA water is separated by chemical means whereas for MAWA water is evaporated. But chemically protein, fat and carbohydrate content of MAWA and CHEENA are same. The heat has made MAWA unhealthy although its chemical means of nutrition is same as CHEENA. Boiling deprives the seed of life-giving capacity. For proper nourishment to dead or inactive organs we need nutrition from live foods like fruits, vegetables not dead food. Cooked food is like dead body as it starts decaying after being prepared. Non-vegetarian foods are even worse than cooked vegetarian food as it starts decay after slaughter.

All our body cells except brain cells are replaced. But God did not make our metabolism such that new cells should be diseased. So, our replaced cells should be diseased free. This is due to our poor lifestyle.

(h) <u>**PLASTIC FOOD-**</u>

What societies eat reflects their position on the modernity, trajectory. Poor countries have health problems because of lack of food. Then as people get rich, they end up losing the health advantage of food availability. They eat processed food, high in salt, sugar and fat, which make themselves ill. Its only when societies get very rich that they discover the benefits of eating real food and value sustainability, but then we realize it's too late.

When we will stop eating plastic food from plastic cans and too then we Indians have our own real food and healthy local cuisines.

(i) <u>MICRONUTRIENTS-</u>

To activate or maintain our body, we need a steady supply of many different raw materials- both micronutrients and macronutrients. We need a large number of macronutrients like- carbohydrates, proteins and fats. And while we only need a small number of micronutrients- like vitamins and minerals.

All cars have wheels, brakes, steerings, body, engines but all cars are not same. It's the minor additions which make all the difference between a good, better and best car. Micronutrients are just like that. Our food plates should have full of colours like a rainbow. The green colour is due to chlorophyll. And the molecular structure of chlorophyll and haemoglobin are same except for Iron in the core of Hemoglobin, that why we emphasis on eating green vegetables. Nearly 30 vitamins and minerals that your body can't manufacture in sufficient amounts on its own are called "essential micronutrients". Some are like milk, yogurt, spinach, broccoli etc.

The key to excellent health and longevity is to eat a high ratio of micronutrients and macronutrients.

(j) <u>MILK-</u>

Boiled milk is not preferable. It's better to have curd instead of milk. An alternative is soya milk. Absolutely milk is a nutrient-packed food having Calcium, Potassium and Vitamin-D. Dairy products can be part of a balanced eating regimen. Milk is not well tolerated by many and has a difficult time digesting it. It also has inflammatory properties. We obtain the same milk properties from seafood, veggies, fruits and nuts. If you do drink milk, because of the hormones and antibiotics fed to the dairy cows, its best to buy organic or grass-fed.

(k) <u>SPROUTS-</u>

The germinated seeds of grains are known as sprouts, and they are known to be healthy food. Most commonly used are moong, chana. However, wheat, methi can also be sprouted. They make hair stronger, controls weight helps in digestion, helps to make skin youthful and are a superfood for pregnant women. Best is to have all the varieties of sprouts.

<u>SPIRULINA- Nature's green magic</u>

Spirulina is considered as a superfood due to its excellent nutritional content and health benefits.

Spirulina is high in protein and vitamins, thus making it as a dietary supplement for vegans and vegetarians.

Benefits-

- Can help to lose weight—people who ate spirulina for 3 months showed improvement in their BMI(Body Mass Index)
- Have inflammation-fighting properties.
- Manage diabetes—the antioxidant effect of spirulina is also helpful in treating type 1 diabetes.
- Boosts immune system.
- Improves gut health—spirulina is not rich in fibre, thus it is important to consume high fibre foods with it.

Spirulina is developed as the "food of the future" because of its ability to synthesize high quality concentrated food more efficiently than any other algae.

National Aeronautics Space Administration (NASA) scientists from the USA tested and found that 1 kg of spirulina is nutritionally equal to 1000 kg of assorted fruits and vegetables.

(I) <u>ACIDIC VS ALKALINE FOODS-</u>

When you eat, the calories and nutrients are extracted from foods and they are metabolized, leaving behind an ash residue. This ash residue determines the pH of the food as acid-forming or alkalinizing food. Cereals, milk products, dals are acidic foods, while fruits and vegetables are alkaline. Fruits clean the food and vegetables build the body.

It's a misconception that potato is fattening. It has 80% water and is too porous, hence can absorb a lot of fat without showing. It should always be taken with the skin. Fruits are predigested foods, hence should be taken one hour before or after the meal. Salads should be taken before the meal, as the time required to digest is much lower.

(m) <u>SUGAR, SALT AND FAT-</u>

In grocery stores and supermarkets, food sections mainly divided into 2 categories- **A-** fresh foods includes fruits and vegetables, which keeps body healthy and **B-** processed foods or the readymade foods contains excessive amount of salt, sugar and fat.

SUGAR-

Sweeteners like jaggery, honey, misri are nutritious. But sugar has only calories. Sugar is taken for taste only. Excess sugar can lead to weight gain and an increased risk of heart disease. Sugar contained diets can increase oil production, androgen secretion which lead to developing acne, accelerate skin ageing.

TABLE SALT-

If you have a high blood pressure problem, doctors are talking about table salts, the table salt is scratching the linings and they start to bleed, so now cholesterol goes there to stop it from bleeding so that you don't bleed to death internally. So now cholesterol is the reason to cause high BP because it narrows the blood vessels and the cholesterol can be absorbed later on. Salt rarely required for nutrition. But salt maybe required replenishing for people who sweat too much like working in hot conditions. It's good to take sea salt because we need salt, we need electricity for body functions.

FAT-

Fried foods, in any case, are bad because of heat exposure. Frying medium needs to be replenished; otherwise the food may become poisonous. Sustained high temperature changes the character of fat making it almost a poison. Fats are almost necessary and must form part of diet. Vitamin A and Vitamin D are fat-soluble. In the absence of fat, body may become deficient of vitamin A and D. fat is rich in calories, hence its intake must be limited particularly for those who are not involved in physical labour.

Ghee benefits—

Concern about weight gain and cholesterol make many people avoid ghee. When consumed in the right quantities, neither does ghee cause weight gain nor does it contribute to an increase in cholesterol level.

You can add 1 tsp of ghee to each of the three complete meals: breakfast, lunch and dinner. Eating this much of ghee can be beneficial for women with PCOS, people with heart disease, high blood pressure and inflammatory bowel syndrome.

So an average of 3-6 tsp of ghee is recommended for good health and weight. Make sure that you source ghee from cow milk, preferably prepared at home.

(n) CURD IN WINTER??

Here is what Ayurveda and Science say— during winter it is very important to safeguard ourselves from the submersing temperature by eating appropriate foods. This can be done by having seasonal foods and changing our eating habits.

Our summer favourite curd is difficult to give up as winter get in. it is believed that curd should be avoided during winters as it leads to cold and sour throat. But is it true? Curd contains bacteria, vitamins, minerals, calcium, magnesium, potassium and protein. Then why we should avoid it?

What Ayurveda says—

As per Ayurveda, curd should be avoided during winters as it increases the secretion of mucus. Dahi is Kapha-Kar in nature, so it is difficult for those who have respiratory problems like; cold, cough, and asthma. Thus, Ayurveda advises to avoid curd during winters and especially at night.

What does Science say?

Curd has a lot of good bacteria for the gut. Curd acts as a great immune booster. Having curd in winter days boosts overall health. But people having respiratory issues should avoid curd after 5 PM as it may create mucus. Curd is rich in vitamin C, which is good for cold suffering people. But the curd should be in the room temperature.

So you don't need to ditch your favourite food during winter days. But you can limit your intake and that should be in room temperature.

FOOD THERAPY

6. **<u>FOOD THERAPY-</u>**

Natural foods have gigantic potential to not only prevent but also heal us from diseases.

The food we eat can either help our body system or it can destroy our system completely. For the proper metabolic activity, we require information, which we get from the foods which we take in our day to day life. If we do not get proper information our body will suffer later. Naturally available foods like- fruits, juices, grains, nuts, vegetables, water are enough to heal most of the problems occurring in our body.

We have been taught by our society that we are omnivores, but actually, we are not. A true omnivore eats its prey in raw form but we are not doing so. Even our mouth waters when we see fresh fruits and vegetables on a farm, and these re most acceptable foods for our species. Eating foods that are not acceptable to our body is like fuelling a car that runs on petrol, with diesel. The outcome will not satisfy. We should consume natural fruits on a daily basis as maximum nutrition of any fruit lies just under its skin.

The more we rely upon indigenous foods and eating habits, the more we likely to stay fit, healthy and happy. As local foods are storehouses of healing properties. Our grandmothers used local herbal concoctions at home to treat headache, fever, stomach pain and whatnot.

- ## YOU SHOULD EAT FRUITS EVERYDAY AS-

Grapes — relax your blood vessels
Blueberries — strengthen your heart
Oranges — protect your skin and vision
Apples — helps resist infection
Bananas — boost your energy
Pineapples — relieve arthritis pain
Watermelon — promote weight loss
Cherries — calm your nerves
Strawberries — fight ageing

- ## CHOOSE RIGHT TEA-

Cinnamon tea — for headache
Thyme tea — for cough
Lemon tea — for sore throat
Peppermint tea — for fatigue

- ## LISTEN TO YOUR BODY-

According to Dr Rakhi Mehra, in fever, light *khichdi* allows rest to the digestive system, while enhancing our taste along with igniting the body's metabolism. Similarly, intake of simple *haldi* (turmeric) powder with normal water proves to be very effective in summer for the usual bouts of colds, coughs and throat infections. Black pepper, ginger, clove and holy basil are very effective during winter in cases of common cold or flu. Despite knowing these facts we prefer to take antihistamine drugs, which further exacerbate our sore throat.

- **<u>DIET TIPS</u> (FROM MANY SOURCES)-**

- Coriander juice consumed on an empty stomach reduces cholesterol.

- 10-15 French beans consumed on an empty stomach helps in controlling diabetes.

- 200-300 curry leaves a day are good for controlling blood pressure and diabetes.
- Approximately 150-160 leaves of tulsi can be consumed three to four times a day for any kind of fever.

- One spoon of onion juice is good for dandruff and greying of hair. Onion juice even gets rid of spectacles if its juice is put in the eyes.

- A handful of Mehendi (henna) leaves are good for jaundice and liver-related problems.

- Carrots are good for increasing haemoglobin and for curing cancer.

- Hibiscus or shoe flower can be consumed for stopping excessive bleeding or piles bleeding. The green leaves of the same plant are very helpful in reducing any kind of infection in the body.
- Flaxseeds contain high levels of phytoestrogen. They not only lessen symptoms of menopause but also have positive effects on cholesterol, cognition and digestion.

- Sprinkling half a cup of sunflower seeds into our morning cereal with milk provides more than a hundred per cent of our day's requirement of vitamin-E.

- Research has shown that turmeric, which is used in many Indian curries, when combined with black pepper, improves the bioavailability of this superfood.

- The antioxidant ellagic acid (found in walnuts, raspberries, pomegranates and cranberries) enhances the ability of quercetin (an antioxidant found in apples, grapes, onions and buckwheat) to kill cancerous cells.

- Amla or the Indian gooseberry has high Vitamin- C content, enhances food absorption, balances stomach acids, fortifies the liver, nourishes the brain and mental functioning and supports the heart. It also strengthens the lungs, regulates the elimination of free radicals, enhances fertility, helps the urinary system, improves skin quality and promotes healthier hair.

- Mulethi or liquorice supports liver health and is an antiseptic that helps to calm the stomach. It is also an expectorant and decongestant that can help fight respiratory infections.

- There is some evidence that liquorice in a small amount can be used to decrease sugar cravings. Moreover, it is also known to be beneficial in cases of low blood pressure.

- Aloe vera juice can be good for the digestive system, skin, hair and teeth. It is an antimicrobial, antioxidant and anti-inflammatory and protects us from ultraviolet (UV) radiation.

- In the case of cancer survivors, it provides protection from skin damage after radiation therapy.

- Wheatgrass is packed with a powerful combination of nutrients and has many therapeutic benefits. It is known as complete nourishment.

- The extensive combination of vitamins and nutrients make wheatgrass an exceptional choice to enhance one's well-being. It has antioxidant, antibacterial and anti-inflammatory properties.

- Lemons have a high content of Vitamin- C, regulate the bowels, are antibacterial and have B-complex vitamins, calcium, copper, iron, magnesium, phosphorus, potassium and fibre. They balance our body's chemistry.

Note- these are general guidelines. Everything needs to be customized to suit one's body.

- **<u>Three amazing juice recipes for better health-</u>**

For a complete detox-
Lemon
Ginger
Celery
Kale
Cucumber
Apple

For increased energy levels-
Apple
Cucumber
Kale
Spinach
Lemon

For improved heart health-
Apple
Orange
Beetroot
Kale
Carrot

- **USES OF HONEY FOR CURING DISEASES-**
For cold - 1 tbsp honey
         1 tbsp lemon juice

For detox – 1 cup herbal tea
         1-2 tsp honey

For toothache- 1 tsp cinnamon
         1 tbsp of honey

For cough-   4 tsp lemon
         8 tsp honey

For weight loss- 1 tsp honey
         ½ tsp cinnamon

For sinus-   1 tbsp honey
         2 tbsp apple cider vinegar

As far as superfoods are concerned, green leafy vegetables, fruits and berries, spices as well as other coloured ones, nuts and seeds, apricots all have different enzymes, vitamins, minerals, trace minerals, phytonutrients, micro and macro-nutrients- all are beneficial for health. The more we limit ourselves to only a few superfoods, the less we feed to our body, but we actually require a lot of variety for great health and healing. At last, fruits should be seasonal and fresh and preferably non-GMO and organic.

• <u>NUTRACEUTICALS—</u>

The term "Nutraceutical" combines the word "nutrient" (a nourishing food or food component) with "Pharmaceutical" (a medical drug). The word "Nutraceutical" has been used to describe a broad list of products sold under the premise of being dietary supplements (i.e. a food), but for the expressed intent of treatment or prevention of disease.

-   The product that has been isolated and purified from food and generally sold in medicinal forms not usually associated with food.

-Nutraceuticals are present in most of the food ingredients with varying concentration.

-Concentration, time and duration of supply of nutraceuticals influence human health.

-Manipulating the foods, the concentration of active ingredients can be increased.
-Diet rich in nutraceuticals along with regular exercise, stresses reduction and maintenance of healthy body weight will maximize health and reduce disease risk.

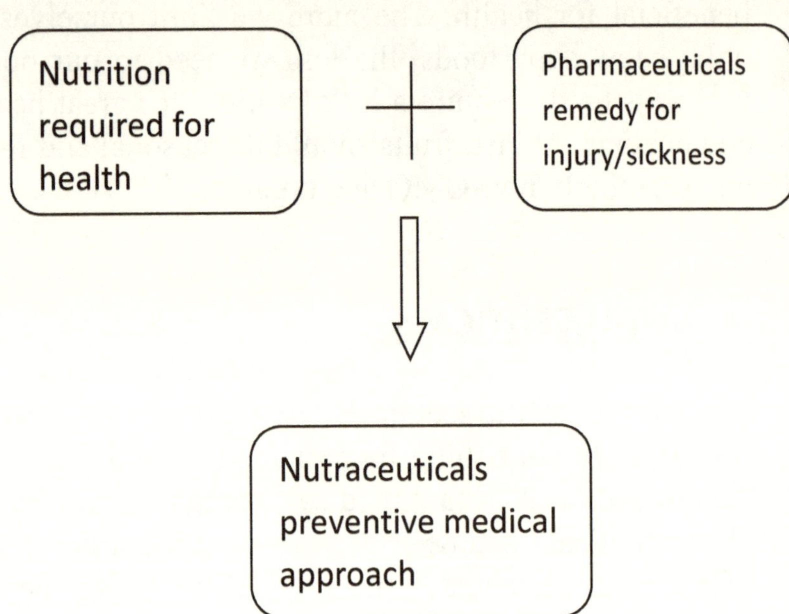

CONCEPT OF NUTRACEUTICALS

Nutraceuticals mainly consist of-

-Nutrients — vitamins, minerals, amino acids, fatty acids.
-Herbals/ Photochemical — herbs, botanical products.

-Dietary supplements — probiotics, prebiotics, antioxidants, enzymes.

• <u>GO WITH YOUR GUT FEELING—</u>

Trillions of bacteria, virus and fungi live inside our body and maintaining a well-balanced relationship with them is to our advantage. Together they form the gut microbiome. A rich ecosystem that performs a variety of functions in our bodies.

The bacteria in our gut can breakdown food that the body can digest producing important nutrients regulate the immune system and protect against harmful germs.

In a recent study, scientists exchanged with regular high fibre diet with a group of South Africans with high-fat meat leafy diets with a group of African Americans. After just 2 weeks on high-fat low fibre western-style diet the South African group showed increased information of the colon, that the short-chain fatty acid that lowers the risk of colon cancer. Meanwhile the group that switched to high fibre low-fat diet had the opposite result. So, what goes wrong with our gut bacteria when we eat low fibre foods? Lower fibre means less fuel for our gut bacteria, essentially starving them. This results in less diversity and hungry bacteria, infect some can even start to feed on mucus living.

In recent microbiome study scientists found that fruits, vegetables, tea, coffee, red wine and dark chocolate are co-related with increased bacterial diversity. These foods contain polyphenol which is naturally occurring antioxidant compounds. On the other hand whole milk and sugary drinks, sodas are co-related with decreased diversity.

Fresh fruits containing more fibre and provide better fuel. So lightly steamed, sorted and raw vegetables are typically more beneficial than fried dishes. There are also ways of preparing foods which introduce good bacteria also called "probiotics".

- ## **PROBIOTICS—**

In ancient Indian society, it became commonplace (and still is) to enjoy a before-dinner yoghurt drink called lassi. These Indian traditions were based on the principle of using milk as a probiotic delivery system to body.

Always talk with your doctor before taking a supplement. These supplements might interfere with medicines you may be taking.

IMPACT OF CHANGE

7. <u>IMPACT OF CHANGE-</u>

Improvement is like adding one drop of colour in a bucket of water daily, nothing visible till a long time. Deterioration is like slow poisoning. So don't get disheartened if improvement takes time to be seen.

The human body has been designed to stay well. We are meant to regenerate and revive ourselves. This only can be discovered if we listen to our physical body, mind and soul and identify our healing mechanism, for we all are indeed unique. It's just like to find our own path, own Gurus, e need to find a follow our own health regimen by observing and analyzing from others in the journey of wellness.

RIGOROUSLY CHANGE IN LIFESTYLE

8. <u>RIGOROUSLY CHANGE IN LIFESTYLE-</u>

It works, & it is more than diet & exercise.

Actually, this powerful medicine exists. It's real and readily available to everyone. It's called intestine lifestyle change. Its ingredients are physical activities and splendid improvements in diet. It works well. If it were an actual pill, no doubt millions of people would be clamoring for it.

Intestine lifestyle changes involve knowledge and action which many doctors think is too difficult to do. Any lifestyle change has to be meaningful and pleasurable. If it's meaningful and pleasurable, people will do it. For these changes to be most effective, people have to want to continue them for the rest of their lives. The physician's job is to act as a coach for the patient, encouraging and guiding their efforts, without judgment.

Everything we eat does one of two things: -

It either nourishes us or poisons us. Food that has been over-processed and contains preservatives acts like slow poison. The entire modern food handling process, where emphasis is on long shelf life, is turning our food into poisons. In order to keep the body healthy, it is fundamental to follow a wholesome diet, consisting of fresh vegetable proteins in the form of lentils, beans, milk products, dried fruits and the like. Besides healthy food, we also need sufficient sleep, fresh air and proper physical exercises, such as yogasanas or other sports.

Learn to live a healthier lifestyle is easy when you change one small thing at a time.

Little changes in diet can lead you to longer life-

To extract maximum benefits, the healthy diet plan must be established earlier in life to improve health in old age and extend lifespan. A decrease in amount of food consumed tends beneficial for the body when they turn old and even gives a boost to longevity.
How can we stay fit in old age for a long time? Researchers into ageing have a simple answer: eat less and healthy.

"One should establish healthy behaviours early in life. It may not be as good for your health to change your diet later in life. Health in old age is a lifelong affair", explains Linda Partridge from the Max Planck Institute for Biology of Ageing.

(a) <u>Pay attention to your body –</u>

If you are hungry, it's because your body isn't getting the nutrients it needs. Give it some. If you are not, there is no reason to force-feed yourself; your body is all set. Never get "full". It confuses your brain because if you are not hungry anymore but you are still eating, you will get a distorted sense of what is "full" is. Eat all the time. If you don't eat until you get very hungry, when you finally get around food, you will end up overeating.

(b) <u>Pay attention to food labels-</u>

Pick foods high in protein & fibre, & low in fat and sugar, especially saturated & trans-fat.

It's okay to eat something unhealthy sometimes, so do not cut your calories if you eat something unhealthy. The heart wants what the heart wants, same for the mouth. If you want to eat a piece of cake, eat one, but give yourself the same amount of nutrients and calories as you would any other day, even if this means you eat a few extra calories that day.

(c) Laughter is the best medicine-

Find something to laugh every day to give your feel-good hormones a boost.

(d)   A right step-

Men and women need 1200 steps a day to control their weight. Invest in a pedometer to make sure you are hitting your target.

(e)   Sunnyside up-

Go outside in the sunshine for a natural boost. The sun' rays on the skin help your body to produce Vitamin-D, which can fight against skin diseases, bone diseases and even some types of cancer.

Giving your partner a hug doesn't just warm the heart, it can protect too. A study by the University of North California found that hugging your other half for 20 seconds could lower blood pressure and reduce levels of the stress hormone cortisol.

EFFECTIVE DIET PLAN

9. <u>EFFECTIVE DIET PLAN-</u>

Here are a few tips to plan your diet effectively and correctly-

There is a myth amongst people that dieting may help you to reduce weight. Although it does not work if not accompanied by proper exercise.

<u>Avoid sugary drinks and fruit juices –</u>

Fruit juices and sugary drinks in tetra packs have added sugar in them, which is toxic to our body; these are the most fattening things you incorporate into your body.

<u>Eat high protein breakfast-</u>

Protein is the most important nutrient for weight loss. The science behind this is that the body uses more calories to metabolize protein, as compared to fats and carbs, and protein also helps to keep you full for a long time.

Drink water an hour before meals-

Keeping yourself hydrated all day is very much necessary. Drinking lots of water not only helps you to lose weight, but it also helps in keeping your skin glowing. It is advised to drink water an hour before your meal as it improves digestion.

Strictly follow your diet plan-

A diet that you plan for your self should be strictly followed for your benefit. Now you know what to eat and what to avoid. Make sure that you follow your diet strictly

HEALTH IS WEALTH

10. <u>HEALTH IS WEALTH-</u>

Spending on healthcare has 2 dimensions preventive and curative. Till now our policy based on curative forms promoting yoga is a preventive strategy, it saves resources and is a good step by the government.

Once upon a time, it was **"Health is Wealth"** and today **<u>"No Health without Wealth"</u>** people are forced to take loans and sells assets for treatment and this is because of the Indian Health Care System.

www.ingramcontent.com/pod-product-compliance
Lightning Source LLC
LaVergne TN
LVHW041748190726
843493LV00008B/2505